GLASSES

WHO NEEDS 'EM?

BY LANE SMITH

PUFFIN BOOKS

To
Salvino d'Armato,
Ben Franklin,
and
Saint Jerome

—*L.S.*

PUFFIN BOOKS
Published by the Penguin Group
Penguin Books Ltd, 27 Wrights Lane, London W8 5TZ, England
Penguin Books USA Inc., 375 Hudson Street, New York, New York 10014, U.S.A.
Penguin Books Australia Ltd, Ringwood, Victoria, Australia
Penguin Books Canada Ltd, 10 Alcorn Avenue, Toronto, Ontario, Canada M4V 3B2
Penguin Books (N.Z.) Ltd, 182–190 Wairau Road, Auckland 10, New Zealand

Penguin Books Ltd, Registered Offices: Harmondsworth, Middlesex, England

First published in the United States of America by Viking 1991
Published in the UK in Picture Puffins 1995

10 9 8 7 6 5 4 3 2 1

ISBN 0-14-055652-4

Made and printed in the United States of America

C150861771

Design: Molly Leach, New York, New York

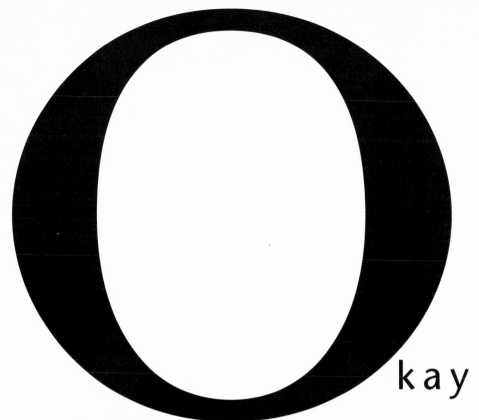

Okay

this was

the situation:

my doctor

said I needed

glasses

.

I told him,
"No way."

He said, "Young man, if
you are worried about
looking a little different..."

I said, "I'm worried
about looking like a wally."

He said, "Lots of folks wear
glasses and love 'em."

He said...

"Your mum wears glasses...

...your dad wears glasses...

...your sister wears glasses..."

"My sister," I said,
"wears green rubber bands
in her hair and T-shirts
with unicorns on 'em."

"Okay then," he said.
"What about famous inventors...

...or 'monster-movie' stuntpeople, hmmm?

Why even *entire planets* wear glasses!"

I thought my doctor might be exaggerating
just a little with that last "planets" statement.
I asked, "Do little green men wear glasses?

Do pink elephants?

Do Hong-Kong-Flu bugs?"

YES!
YES!
YES!

was his answer
(I thought it might be).
He continued...

"...But you left out cats and dogs and
snowmen and robots!" He was very excited.
I was going to suggest maybe he was
putting too much sugar on his cereal...

...but he started up again.
"Giant dinosaurs wear glasses...

...and little worms...

...and tall giraffes...

...and short fuzzy bunnies."

"Well, if you're going to insist on rabbits wearing glasses, maybe we should give some specs to their carrots too!"

"Don't be ridiculous," he answered. "Carrots don't *need* glasses...

...potatoes however..."

"Oh brother, now I understand...
you're a loony aren't you?
I bet you see glasses on cuckoo birds...

...and buffoonish baboons..."

"Now you're catching on...
allow me then to also
point out sheep and opossum
and chameleon and fish

and oil painting

and sock puppet

and chameleon

and crocodile

and chameleon...

They all wear glasses! Oh, and...ahem...

...I do too!"

"You need them," I said.
"You've been seeing things!"
And with that, I started to leave.

"Just a minute, young man...

I told him, "The gold-wire rims will be just fine."